no *perfect* beginning

IMPERFECTION SERIES PREQUEL

Award-winning Author
DD LORENZO

Chapter 1

Carter

No matter where I wind up in this life, this place will always be my favorite. There's a tranquil rhythm that settles my mind when the ocean waves lap against the shore. They echo in perfect harmony with the sunset's golden hues. The colors streak across the sky while a creamy beige carpet of soft, smooth sand stretches out until it meets the sea.

I'm looking forward to this week and to doing morning runs here with Lacey, the woman who holds my heart.

"You look completely lost in thought." She pokes the cap of my arm with her finger. "I'll give you a penny for them," she says in a sweet, sing-song, lyrical kind of voice.

"I was just thinking about how different our morning run will be. I've done both, but I wonder how you'll compare a run on the beach to a run in the mountains. I think both are nice."

"Of course they are, silly man. That's the beauty of living in Maryland. We get both. When one side of the state is mountains, and the other side butts up against the ocean, it's a win/win in my book." She nudges me with her shoulder and flashes a megawatt smile. "By the way, I unpacked. I put your duffle bag on the bed. I know how you like to put your stuff away yourself."

"Thanks," I nod. There are many things I love about this woman, and this is just one more. She gets me. Like, really gets me. I have a deep-seated need for order, and Lacey has no problem with it.

I can't remember a time when my mind wasn't consumed with a burning need for structure. I don't know if it was there when I was born, but it came to life when my parents split up. As a kid of twelve, having my world turned upside down detonated something inside of me. Something that blew apart any carefree and impulsive thoughts. From that point forward, I needed order. Predictability. A world where very little went askew. My brain dictates rituals, most of which have to do with staying safe. Lock doors and windows. Make sure the stove is off before we leave the house. Mundane tasks that give me peace of mind. That same love of order made me search for a stint in the military and a career as a State Trooper, where it's necessary for order to reign.

As a teenager, some recommended treatment for my obsessive thoughts and compulsive behaviors. I disagreed, and my mother didn't insist that I do so. The divorce felt heavy and dark to me, not to mention out of my control. Structure helped. I think my mom welcomed having a kid who kept his room clean and insisted on doing his own laundry. There's no mistaking it was a trying time for her when my old man up and decided out of nowhere he didn't want a family. There was never a hint. Never a glimpse that he was unhappy. One day, he was playing football with my brother in the backyard, and the next, he told Mom he was leaving. When she asked him why, he gave no reason. Then he was gone, leaving her to take care of two boys alone to pick up the pieces of a world he'd shattered.

From that day, I sought an existence of stable force. On some level, I think Mom understood. In light of such unpredictable circumstances, I think she welcomed a little stability in her kid. She doesn't mind my ways—then or now—and Lacey doesn't either.

"If you want to help your Mom get settled, I don't mind unpacking for you."

I press my lips into a smile. "I got it, babe."

She gives me a knowing smile and then looks away, enjoying the view on our first day of vacation. The woman is one of a kind, and I can't imagine a day without her adding brightness to my shadows. Hopefully, this week, she'll agree to add even more permanence to my life when I ask her to be my wife.

As she and I watch the waves crash against the shore, a sense of calm washes over me. The salty sea breeze fills my lungs, and I truly feel at peace with those who matter—my mother, brother, and love of my life—nearby; the static inside my head smooths, and the ever-present knots in my gut unravel.

Lacey's touch awakes my inner thoughts as her fingers intertwine with mine. She has no idea how her touch grounds me and keeps me in the present moment. A deep, coffee-rich rumble rolls through the air, and I glance toward the screen door. My kid brother—Mr. Eye Candy himself—is laughing at some comment our mom made. A sense of comfort and family falls over me as it hits me that, for the next week, I'll enjoy the people I love most in a place that's as familiar as an old friend.

"You want to run with us in the morning?" I ask Declan through the screen door. "Since we have a week, I thought we might hit all the towns; Ocean City, Fenwick, Bethany, Rehoboth, Lewes ... for a change of pace."

"I'm down for it," Declan answers from inside the house.

"And I'm up for it," Lacey chimes in. She busses a kiss on my cheek. "I'm going to go help your mom put away the groceries."

"Okay."

I watch as she disappears through the creaky screen door. It feels as if she's always been a part of this routine, though this is her first time here. We've stayed in this cottage every year for as long as I can remember. It's an Ocean City original and has changed little in the twenty-some-odd years Mom's been bringing us here. Me and my brother agree this house holds some of our best and most treasured memories. This is the first time I've ever brought someone along with us, but then, Lacey isn't just "someone."

"Brought you a beer." The screen door moans as my brother pushes his shoulder against it. It slams loudly once he's passed the frame.

"Thanks." I take the bottle, twist off the top, then take a long swig. The frosty glass is already sweating from the leftover August humidity.

I grab one of the old Adirondack chairs by the arm and drag it to a place where it'll be easy to prop my feet up on the railing. Lacey appears and follows my lead, pulling a chair of her own next to mine while Declan plants his ass down on the railing. "I thought you were helping Mom?"

Lacey leans back and pulls her hair up into a quick, messy bun. "She said she didn't need help and that she'd be out in a few minutes. She's washing the dishes and the pots and pans," she says, amused.

I nudge a shoulder toward my ear. "She always does that."

"Seems the apple doesn't fall far from the tree in some respects," she responds.

"Mom cleans them to her standards," I explain with an air of nonchalance. "It's either that or she'd be insisting on packing up her kitchen and bringing it with her."

"I guess," she says again in that knowing, sing-song tone.

"You, of all people, would understand," Declan interjects.

"She says she likes to cook for her boys and wants to make sure they don't pick up any germs," Lacey informs.

Declan and I exchange a look. "Riiiiiiight." We both laugh as we chime the word in unison.

"We know better. The woman is militant when it comes to cleaning things." Declan says.

"Well, she isn't hurting anyone," I defend. "And she

doesn't really get the chance to do much cooking anymore. Besides, she likes doing it."

Declan shakes his head in disbelief. "Why is she cooking on her vacation, anyway? All three of us work. We should be taking her out to dinner."

I shrug off my brother's comment. "Everybody's got their thing, Declan. Leave her be."

I look over at Lacey, who's now come to Mom's defense. She's so damn cute in her cut-off shorts and tank top. She settles back into her chair and lets out a contented sigh. The breeze gently blows a few loose strands of her hair, and when she leans her head back, she closes her eyes and breathes in a deep lungful of the tranquility known as vitamin sea.

"I can feel you staring at me," she says, her eyes still closed.

"I can't help myself," I admit. I love every inch of her and have since the moment we met. Her long blonde hair, now captured in that erratic topknot, cascades typically down her back in loose waves when not pulled into a runner's style ponytail. Her sun-kissed skin glows in the golden light of the lowering sun. It's hard to believe that little more than a year ago, we were complete strangers. Our blind date, set up by mutual friends, led me to my fate.

Her eyes open wide, the gorgeous emerald color reminding me of Springtime at the lake when everything comes to life. She tips her head and smiles at me. "It's peaceful here." Her expression mirrors the feeling in my soul.

I couldn't have guessed that date would lead me to the girl I'd one day want to marry—not that she ever had a clue. I study her face, losing myself in her eyes. Before this week is over, I'm going to propose to her and ask my brother to be my best man.

Chapter 2

Lacey

Watching my parent's shitty marriage, and living with my own idiosyncrasies, had all but turned me off from the idea of marriage. It's incredible how one person can come into your life and completely change your perspective. Before Carter, I was content to focus on my career as a teacher. But now, I can't imagine my life without him.

He interrupts my thoughts for just a moment as he takes my hand and presses a kiss to the back of it. His eyes meet mine, and I revel in how cherished he makes me feel and how happy I am.

"I love you, woman."

My smile widens, and he leans in to press a soft

kiss to my mouth. "I love you, too," I whisper against his lips. The man makes my heart feel full to bursting.

"Would you knock it off?" Declan playfully chides. "You're making me sick with all this lovey-dovey crap."

Carter's brother breaks through the sweet moment, and we turn to see him rolling his eyes and pursing his lips. He loves to give us shit.

"You're just jealous," I accuse.

"You're making me nauseous," he jokes with a flattened tone.

"Declan, pull up a chair for me." Rose smiles as she comes through the doorway. Perched in her hand is a glass of wine. She waits as her son does her bidding, and I smile. A pang of bittersweet emotion washes over me as the sucker punch of my own loss hits below the belt, so to speak. It hasn't been easy for Rose, and it's bearing witness to moments like these I cherish. Rose has become such a dear friend. She's overcome so much raising two boys alone. She joins our group and takes a seat. Her relaxed expression warms my heart. I wish moments like these could last forever, frozen in time like a cherished photograph. It's a nice thought, but I'm a realist. I'm well aware life is ever-changing, like the seasons, and always moving forward.

As Rose relaxes in her seat, the sky morphs into cotton candy with soft shades of pink and blue. I whisper to Carter, "I'm so glad we have this time together."

"Me, too," he answers, squeezing my hand. "It feels good to be here with family."

Never in a million years did I expect to hook up with a cop, but, as in many things, Carter Sinclair is an exception.

Willow Acres wasn't exactly the nicest place to grow up. In the trailer park, most did what they could to avoid the police. The majority of kids who lived there got in trouble with the law by the time they'd reached their teenage years. I was the exception. My mother wanted better opportunities for me than she'd had for herself, so my upbringing was strict. Mom put great importance and heavy emphasis on my schooling. Lucky for her, I loved to learn. She instilled in me a passion for education along with a heaping dose of ambition. Her efforts paid off. I never fell into the pitfalls suffered by my peers. I suppose every decent parent wants their child to do at least one step better than they did, and by the time I reached my junior year of high school, offers for university scholarships came rolling in. It seemed only fitting that I go into teaching.

I'd saved enough money from waitressing jobs to afford to move into a small apartment of my own. It wasn't far from the high school where I accepted a teaching position. Carter was the love story I never saw coming.

A few months into the school year, a teacher friend named Julie set me up on a blind date. Only after I insisted I wouldn't meet alone with a total stranger did she arrange for her and her husband to join us. Her husband, Ken, was a Trooper, and Carter was their friend. Julie told me three things about Carter. One, he was a Trooper. Two, he was handsome. Third, he lived on the lake.

From the moment I met him, I knew he was different than anyone I'd met before. He had this aura of strength about him that enveloped me as he approached. It wasn't intimidating. It was more like a sense of protection I had never felt in Willow Acres.

His tall frame towered over my petite one. He was unbelievably handsome, with sharp features that demanded my attention. His cheekbones and jaw were exquisitely cut, and he was impeccably groomed. He exuded authority like the scent of cologne, and the intensity in his gaze uncloaked a seriousness I found sorely lacking in most men I'd met.

Within the first few minutes of our meeting, he checked all my boxes. His confidence and charm blended with his good looks. We discussed politics and current events and how we pictured our futures. As we grew to know each other better, we learned we had more in common than just our love of good food. Like me, he was a runner. We started with one run a week, then two, then more.

When Carter took me to Baltimore to meet Rose, Declan was visiting their mother. It didn't take long for me to recognize that the face of Ralph Lauren and Gucci ads was, in reality, my boyfriend's bratty little brother. I loved their interaction. Little by little, I learned of all they'd been through together, and it explained Carter's intensity, Declan's need for attention, and their loyalty to each other and Rose. They defined the word family, and when I lost my mother, they taught me that not all families share a bloodline.

"How are you doing, sweetheart?" Rose gives me a sweet smile.

"I'm good. I like it here. How about you? How are you feeling? You put in a full day's work in that kitchen."

"I'm fine." Rose's cheeks are slightly flushed, but I'm guessing it's more from the wine than the work. "This is a good place. We love it here."

I follow her gaze to the ocean and the pastel sky, which is changing as quickly as if it were a kaleidoscope. "I'm so glad Carter invited me."

"Me, too. I love my boys, but it's nice to have another woman to talk to. She steals a glance at them as she lowers her voice. "They can be a real pain in the butt sometimes if you know what I mean."

I nod and then am distracted as Carter clears his throat. "I heard that, Mom."

I savor the sweet tang of the salty sea breeze as I close myself off from their banter.

Chapter 3

Carter

We're interrupted by the approach of a tall woman with exotic features. The closer she gets to me, the clearer my vision, and I recognize her as someone who's been in several commercials with Declan. He waves to her.

"C'mon up," he calls.

"What's her name?" I ask as my gaze snaps from her to him.

"Her name is Marisol. Marisol Franzi. We work together."

My spine stiffens as Declan extends his hand to her. She takes it, and the hair on my neck rises. I wasn't expecting a guest.

"Everyone, this is Marisol. Marisol, this is my mom,

Rose, my brother, Carter, and Carter's better half, Lacey."

A pregnant pause follows as she inspects us. "It's nice to meet you."

My ass.

Her tone is condescending, and her manner superior. My gaze drifts from her to my brother. He can tell I'm not happy. "We weren't expecting guests."

"I didn't think anyone would mind if she joined us for dinner," Declan announces.

I give him a stern look. "It would have been nice if you would've given us a heads-up. I'm not sure we're prepared for guests."

Declan shrugs me off. "I didn't think it was that big a deal. You have Lacey here. I thought I'd invite a friend as well."

Of course you did.

As usual, the typical youngest child asks no permission but expects forgiveness. The I can do what I want and get away with it attitude of childhood screams entitlement now that he's an adult. If you have this, I can have that. It's bullshit. I'm about to say something snarky, the words ready to rapidly fire from my lips, when Mom rises from her chair and cuts in front of me.

"It's very nice to meet you. Marisol, did you say? What a lovely name." Mom reaches for her hand. "I'm Rose."

"You're the mother, correct?"

A smile I can only describe as villainous slinks onto Marisol's lips, and her gaze drifts between the three of us. She looks up, her surveilling eyes settling on Declan.

"It's so strange. I see no resemblance at all." She pauses, the smile turning a bit more wicked as she sets her eyes on Mom. "He's adopted?"

My mother's smile crumbles as her eyes widen. She's momentarily stunned. I'm not.

"What a curious thing to say to someone you've just met. If my mother wasn't so understanding, she might take it as an insult. Since you're a guest of my brother's, I'll give you a little leeway. Maybe something got lost in translation. He's not adopted though, at the moment, he might as well be." I turn my sight to Declan. "Your friend's manners need checking."

"She didn't mean it as an insult," Declan interjects. "Sometimes things do get lost in translation. Marisol's originally from Columbia."

"Oh, no. I meant ... Declan's a very handsome man. He doesn't look like either of you."

My forehead pinches. "Wow. They must not have manners in Columbia. The insults just keep on coming with you, huh? Maybe you should think about what you're saying before you open your mouth."

"Knock it off, Carter," Declan spits.

"Muzzle your guest, Declan."

"Stop it," Mom interjects. "I'm sure it's just a misunderstanding." She issues Marisol a sweet smile. "Are you staying nearby, dear?"

"Dee-clan invited me—"

"She's staying here." Declan drops.

"We don't have the room."

"She can stay in my room."

Heat fires up my neck. "I don't think so." I cast a look at Marisol. "But since my brother got you here on false pretenses, you're welcome to stay for dinner."

The two of us exchange a heated glance. I could kick my brother's ass for ruining our first day here because he's so goddamn cocky.

Marisol looks between us. By the look in her eyes, she's no doubt enjoying the tension. Her sinister smile widens. "Miscommunication is a problem even when language isn't a barrier, no?"

I shoot a look at my brother. "Straighten this out, Dee-clan."

"I did. She's staying."

"Like hell she is." I'm about to go nuclear on his ass when Marisol interjects.

"Aww. I love it when men fight over me."

I've had enough of this shit.

Everyone is quiet as I rise and go inside the house. I grab my cell phone, look up the number of a hotel downtown, and dial. "Yeah, I'd like to make a reservation ..."

"Declan!"

The porch door whines as he enters the house. "What?"

"I just texted reservation details for Marisol to your phone."

He rears back. "What? You don't even know her schedule."

I slip the cell into my back pocket. "I don't give a shit about her schedule. It's for two nights. King room. You can alter it when you take her there."

He challenges me with a dagger-filled stare. "What is your problem? You're being rude."

"Me? Rude?" I scoff. "That's rich. Your girlfriend gave us all a hefty dose. She's not staying here."

"She's not my girlfriend, and I'm not a little kid you can boss around."

He's plucked my last nerve.

I fly at his face, teeth gritted and nostrils flared. "I said ... Marisol's. Not. Staying."

We exchange angry glares, then Declan's expression turns cocky. He shrugs. "You made the plans. You tell her."

"I will."

"I'm warning you; she's got a nasty temper."

"All the better that she has somewhere to spew it." I stomp out to the porch, where my mother makes an attempt at small talk with Marisol. Lacey watches as I insert myself in between the two women.

"Excuse me, Mom. I've made reservations for Marisol at the Marriott downtown. "I turn to Marisol. "Declan will drive you. I booked two nights. It's a nice hotel, though I'm sure the accommodations won't be what you're used to."

She eyeballs me with a narrow-eyed glance. I can almost see the moment when it dawns on her that I'm not playing because the sinister smile returns.

"Thank you." She turns her eyes to Declan. "Thank you for your offer to stay, Dee-clan, but I must take your brother's offer instead. Of course, you're welcome to stay. We always have a good time, don't we."

It's a statement, not a question, and she runs her hand down Declan's arm in a seductive move.

A huffed laugh escapes. This bitch acts like she's in heat, and my mother's eyes widen. She's not naive. Declan hasn't lived at home for a couple of years. His virginity isn't in question. It's Marisol's behavior that surprises Mom. She's bold. No, not bold; vulgar. Where most women would want to keep their private lives private, she seems to thrive on the shock value her behavior incites.

"Maybe you should take Marisol out to dinner, brother. Get her something to eat." His eyes meet mine, and a sneer finds its way to my lips. "I mean, seriously, Dec, the woman looks like she hasn't had a good meal in ages."

Chapter 4

Lacey

An awkward silence falls as Declan and Marisol depart. Once they're gone, Carter heads inside the house. I follow behind him until we're in the kitchen.

"Why did that woman being here make you so upset?" I ask as he fetches another beer from the refrigerator.

Carter closes the fridge door, his hip smacking against the counter as he twists the cap off as if he's strangling it. He looks away from me, chucks the top into the trash can, and takes a long swig from the bottle before meeting my eyes.

"Should I ask you again?" I pry.

"This week's for family. She's not family." His tone

is flat, belying the emotion I know is raging inside of him.

"Stop. Declan could say the same thing about me, but he didn't put up a fuss about my being here."

He levels me with his stare. "You're more family than she is."

"Still, the fact remains, I'm not. I have no more right to be here than Marisol."

Carter reaches for my hand and pulls me in, pressing a soft kiss to my lips. "Don't compare yourself to her."

"I'm not. It's obvious who's worldly and who's not." She's a model, and I'm ... not."

He releases me and walks away. He yanks a chair from the table and plops into the seat. I do the same but in a gentler manner. "What's really bugging you?"

"She's an entitled bitch. Didn't you notice how she acted like she was better than us? She acted like she was doing us a favor by being here, and she insulted my mother. There's no fucking cause for that, Lacey. She's not welcome here. Besides, she never set foot in the house, and I could see the distaste in her eyes by the way she looked at it. It was obvious she'd be more comfortable elsewhere, so I set it right for her."

"I don't think that's true," I scoff.

"Bullshit, Lace. Let's face it; this house is run down

with creaks and cracks, but it's special. It's been good enough for us for years."

"I'm sure she would have loved it once she let her hair down. Besides, it's the people you're with, not the house, that make a great vacation."

"Which is another reason why Declan shouldn't have brought her here. She doesn't fit in."

"Did you give her a chance?"

"She didn't deserve one."

He looks away. I savor the momentary reprieve.

"Hey. Look at me." He lets out an exasperated sigh as his eyes meet mine. I reach across the table and touch his hand. "You're a cop. Isn't everyone supposed to be innocent until proven guilty? Of course, she's different. She's from another culture."

"So, now you're defending her?" He pulls his hand away.

"I'm just saying, maybe he invited her so he wouldn't feel like a third wheel. Maybe he just wanted some company."

He smirks. "And now you're defending him."

"I'm just trying to play devil's advocate."

"Don't."

Rose enters the room, and we stop talking. She looks between the two of us, gauging the situation before she speaks. She then comes over to where we're sitting, pulls out a chair across from Carter, and takes a seat.

"Your brother's upset."

Carter looks at her, and his brows perk. "He'll get over it." He lifts the bottle to his lips and takes another drink.

Rose drifts back into the chair, seemingly deflated. "I was really hoping for a peaceful vacation."

Carter's forehead pinches. "That's on him, Mom, not me."

"Your brother's taking Marisol to the hotel. When he comes back, I'd like the two of you to smooth this over. I don't want arguing."

"I'm not arguing with him, Mom. It's good, as far as I'm concerned."

Carter's indifferent shrug elicits an exasperated sigh from his mother. There's a pained look on her face. I can almost feel the gut twists.

"You might not say the words, Carter, but I know you; that chip on your shoulder won't serve any of us well."

He throws his hands up in a move of disgust.

"I love how you're making this my fault. What do you want from me? I'm not the one who brought someone to our vacation unannounced."

"And that upset your apple cart," Rose interjects. "I get it. I know you, but I'm asking you to let this slide."

"Look, Mom ... Declan knew what he was doing. He just thought he'd work his charm and squeeze it through."

"What if this is our last vacation together?"

Carter freezes. "What? Why would you say that?"

Rose shakes her head. "I'm just saying, with him in New York and you up at Deep Creek, we don't often get time together. Whatever time we spend—especially when we're on vacation—I'd like to add this experience to all our other ones here. Making good memories. Not fighting. Could you please try to be nice to your brother?"

"I'm always nice to my brother."

"No, you're not. You always have each other's backs, but you aren't always nice."

A resigned look of disgust fills Carter's expression. "As long as he keeps that bitch on a leash, I'll be fine."

"Is that any way to talk about your brother's friend?" She pauses. "He'll probably invite her over, and she came all the way from New York to keep Declan company. We can all be polite."

"Sure, Mom. Whatever you say." He tosses me a quick glance. "Remind me to get a big bottle of Tums. I might have a little trouble stomaching her."

Just then, the screen door slams and an angry Declan enters the room. He marches right over to Carter.

"Now that Marisol is gone tell me, what the hell was that all about?"

Chapter 5

Carter

Tension thickens the air.

"Why, whatever do you mean, brother?" I feign innocence.

"What is your problem with Marisol?"

"Oh, you mean the vile person you sprung on us. I don't know what you're talking about." I look over at my mother. "How's that for letting it go, Mom?"

"For God's sake, Carter, can you pull your head out of your ass? I know you like to have everything planned down to the minute, but I invited her, and you treated her like shit."

"Sorry 'bout that."

"No, you're not. You didn't like Marisol from the moment she arrived."

"Gut instinct."

"From a five-minute visit?"

"What can I say? Her superior attitude was shining through."

I can't help the sarcasm.

"I'll give you that; she's a little uppity. Still, it's no reason to be rude—and you were. You were an arrogant ass and a bully."

I shrug off the comment and look away, still incensed that no one but me seems to have a healthy respect for our plans.

Declan throws his hands up. "Fine. I'll go stay with her."

"What? No." Mom intervenes.

"I can't just abandon her, Mom. It wouldn't be right. She's here because of me, and she doesn't know anyone or anything about the area."

"But I don't want you to," Mom pleads, her crestfallen expression getting both of our attention.

"He wants to, can't you tell? He was probably just looking for an excuse. Well, there you go. I gave you one." I snarl, feeling a surge of anger.

"What is wrong with you?" He gives me a puzzled look. "We are not little kids, and you're not the fucking camp counselor."

"Declan! Language!" The harsh word catches Mom off guard.

"I can't help it. Carter's being completely unreasonable, not to mention controlling." Frustration is thick in his tone.

"Is that why you didn't tell anyone about her? Because you knew I wouldn't want a complete stranger here?"

He gives me a look of disbelief. "What? No. I didn't think it was that big a deal. I just wanted a friend to hang out with."

"Yeah, right," I mutter. "A friend," I say the words under my breath but not low enough so Declan doesn't hear them.

"She is a friend, asshole," Declan retorts, rolling his eyes and shaking his head. "She had a driver bring her down because I told her she might have fun." He looks away and inhales a deep breath. "And, oh, what fun it's been so far!" He rolls his eyes and throws his hands around in an animated motion.

Everyone stares at me. I look away in disgust. "I'm always the bad guy."

"Look, you and Lacey ... I just thought it might be fun. That the four of us could hang out."

"And do what? 'Diva Denise' doesn't look like she even owns a pair of flip-flops."

"I don't know. Hit up Seacrets ... have a few drinks ... listen to a few bands."

"And you think she'd be into that? She's a fish out

of water. We're all barefoot and sandy, and she's in stilettos. She would have looked more comfortable wearing bubble wrap."

"And you got all of that from that brief meeting?" Declan scoffs. "You're impossible."

"It's a gift," I snarl.

Declan's spine stiffens as he throws me a deadly glare. "You know, the double standard is getting old. You're judgmental and rigid, and you apply it to everyone and everything. You think I don't know you? You not only judged her the minute you saw her, but you also didn't like that she didn't fit into the plan. You talk about entitled? What about you? You think all of us should just go along with our OCD and not say anything. Well, guess what? I judge you for that. You know you have a problem, and instead of fixing it, you expect all of us to live with it. Not me. Not anymore. Fuck you, and fuck your need for control. If you ask me, you're the one who's entitled. You get to do and say what you want, and we're all supposed to play by your rules."

"Stop! Just stop!" Mom's plea splits the air.

"See what you did?" Declan's question is a conviction.

"I didn't do shit, and I resent the implication. Go back to your fuck buddy." I spit the conviction back at him.

"She's not my fuck buddy!" Declan steps toward me with a clenched fist.

"Just stop it!" Lacey's voice cracks with anger. "Enough." She shoots us both a piercing look, and her tone cuts the tension like a sharp blade. We've hit a trifecta, it seems; anger, disappointment, and hurt.

Instantly, I feel the weight of my actions. Mom's right: I did have a chip on my shoulder, but it graduated to the size of a boulder. No one knows what I have planned, yet I'm holding Declan responsible in advance for disrupting it. As I look at Lacey, her arms wrapped around my mother, whose cheeks are damp with tears, I feel sick to my stomach and full of remorse.

"Sorry, Mom." Declan's voice drops, and his tone is filled with sorrow.

"Sorry," I echo.

Mom's shoulders tremble as she stares down at her lap.

"I didn't ..." I look away, disgusted with myself.

"I know," she says softly. "Can we please just let this go and try to have a good week together?" She sniffles, and Lacey grabs a box of tissues from the counter. "Thank you." Mom pulls a few from the box and gives Lacey a forced smile. She wipes her eyes and wipes her nose, then looks up. Her gaze travels between my brother and me. "I'd like you two to work this out. For me."

The room falls silent as the weight of her words hits us. Mom doesn't ask much, and when she does, it's rarely for herself.

Instantly, I attempt to make amends, but words seem to fail me, and Declan is the one who breaks the silence.

"This isn't about Marisol or me. It isn't even about me bringing her here. This is about the order in your head, Carter, and I get it. We all get it. One thing doesn't go according to plan, and it does something chaotic to your brain. While I might not understand it, I know how it affects you, and I should recognize it for what it is. But it affects us all. You gotta give us a little room to breathe, brother. If you want to keep a tight rein on yourself, that's fine, but you can't put that rope around all of our necks. You're choking the joy out of everything."

Chapter 6

Lacey

I need a reprieve from the tension. I leave Carter and Declan with Rose and escape outside. While the three of them huddled at the table, I grabbed a beer. The setting sun has given way to an inky dark sky. As I pinch the long-neck bottle and bring it to my lips, I look out at a night sky filled with hundreds of stars. I inhale deeply. It doesn't take long before the tension unravels, and a sense of ease lengthens my muscles.

The screen door slams.

"Where's your mother?" I ask as Carter comes up alongside me.

"Laying down."

His answer was short, but so was my question. I'm not feeling particularly lovable toward him right now—or toward Declan, for that matter. He and his brother acted like two little brats, and they really pissed me off.

"What's the problem, Lace? You might as well spit it out now." He's curt.

"Lose the attitude, Carter." I turn, impatience rolling off me. "It is amazing to me that you feel so challenged—dare I say, even threatened—by Marisol. And don't tell me it's just that she's an 'unexpected' wrench in your plans. You resent her being here, but more than that, you resent her."

"Now, this is a first," he says as he draws his spine toward the back of the chair. "I would have thought you, of all people, wouldn't like someone so pretentious."

"Why 'me' of all people?"

"Because women like her always look down on women like you."

"Excuse me?" My eyes go wide. "Women like me?"

"Stop." He gives me a disapproving shake of his head and a look of warning. "You know what I mean. Don't take it out of context."

My head cocks, and my eyes narrow. "Why don't you explain it to me like I'm five years old, and you don't want to hurt my feelings."

"Great. Just great." He looks away.

"I'm serious."

"Okay, you're unpretentious. You're practical. You aren't into the manicured nails and the fancy hair."

"Oh, really. And that makes Marisol what, exactly?"

"I don't know ... glamorous. Extra. Designer. High maintenance."

"Okay, then." I turn away from him and take a very long drink.

He looks at me with a blank stare. "So, what is the problem? It was a compliment."

"I suppose you would think that telling me I'm not glamorous is a compliment. You need to work on those wooing skills, Carter. They're a bit below par."

He plops his feet up on the rail. "I do NOT understand females."

"You got that right."

"First, Mom. Now you. Is it so much to ask for an easy vacation? That people and things can stay the way they're supposed to be and be appreciated as such?"

"No, it isn't too much to ask, but sometimes, plans change ... and sometimes change is better."

"Okay. Enlighten me; let's go to the subject of Marisol."

"Okay. Go."

"I get gut feelings about people, and the one I get from her isn't good. She's not our kind of people. She's arrogant, high falutin', and patronizing. She's snobby, cocky, and seems a bit bossy. She's—"

"Stop. I get it."

"So, tell me, how could a week with a woman who defines the word 'bitch' be a change for the better."

My brows quirk. "Declan is right; you are judgy."

"It wasn't hard." His forehead wrinkles. "She walked in here like she was the fucking queen."

"But you have no idea who she is or what her culture is like ... You know nothing about her."

He looks away. "Pfft. I know enough."

"Now, who's being the snob?" I huff.

His jaw clenches as he stares out into the pitch. I take a deep breath as I rein in my frustration. Maybe my nerves are raw because it's been a hell of a long day. The drive was around seven hours in total. Packing up ourselves and then Rose ... it made for a long trip. The unexpected Marisol and Rose crying. I'm tired. I don't get frazzled like Carter, and even I'm feeling the strain. Now this ... But he loves me.

I let go of the tension and let the serene sound of soft waves take me to a place of simplicity. Carter's protective and annoyingly orderly. Sometimes, it's suffocating, but it also can feel comforting to have someone else in control.

"I get it. You're worried about upsetting the family dynamic. But Marisol isn't the enemy here. She's just different." My words are soft and gentle to get through the defenses I'm sure he's put up.

He runs his hand through his hair and exhales a deep sigh. "It's just that everything was planned. I don't want anything to get more complicated than it is." He avoids my gaze, vacantly staring off. "I've been looking forward to all of us being together for so long."

I sigh. I can't imagine what it feels like to be inside Carter's head. To crave consistency and order in all things, and to feel like someone drops all the marbles when that sequencing isn't present.

Feeling both my anger and his frustration abating in the placidity of the evening, we sit in companionable silence as the night air envelops us in a comfortable, cool embrace.

"Let's try to give Marisol a chance, okay? For Declan's sake. Maybe she isn't as bad as your gut is telling you. Maybe the supermodel thing hasn't gone to her head, and she's just a simple girl."

"Yeah, right," he chuckles. "My gut hasn't failed me yet when it comes to first impressions. I don't know why it would start now."

"C'mon. Humor me," I coax. "After all, your brother is the hottest thing in modeling, and he's still just

Declan. No matter how big a billboard he's on, nothing's going to change that."

Carter smiles at me. He stands and holds out his hand.

"What?" I ask, feeling coy.

"Stand up and take my hand."

It's so still. The quiet scene blends with the alcohol, and when I stand, I feel a little off balance. He catches my hand and pulls me into him, then sways.

"What are you doing?"

"Dancing." His arm comes around my waist.

"There's no music." Our eyes lock, and I fall into the tenderness I see there.

"Sure, there is. Hear it?"

I catch my bottom lip with my teeth. "All I hear is the ocean."

"That's it. It's playing just for us."

We rock back and forth, moving with small, incremental steps in a circular motion.

"Someday, when I'm awfully low ..."

I smile. "You're singing my favorite song from my favorite movie."

"I know. My Best Friend's Wedding."

"And the Tony Bennett version. Not Frank's."

"The moment I met you, my gut said, 'This one's special.' I've never second-guessed that first impression."

"No? Not even because I'm so plain?"

"You aren't plain. You're the girl next door. An all-American beauty. Natural. Perfect."

"Now, you're flattering me."

"It's the truth, and I'm telling you because I love you."

He kisses me, and the world falls away.

Chapter 7

Carter

Sleep escapes me, and the little rest I did get did nothing to squelch the remorse I feel. I royally screwed up yesterday, and I should have let it go, but now I have to rearrange plans.

When Declan went up to bed, I sensed he was still pissed off at me. And I made my mother cry. Shit. I made my mother cry.

I think I have a problem.

It's up to me to fix this.

It always has been.

Fixing it when I was younger meant being the perfect kid. Keeping the stress low when my parents argued and when my father left.

It was easier when I was a kid, I think. Good grades. Not doing things other kids did to get into trouble. I remember right before my dad left. It was a Friday night. I was twelve, almost thirteen. He said, "No friends to hang with on a Friday night, huh, kid? I guess that's because you're such a nerd." It was the first time I remember being consumed by anger. It raged through me like an inferno. "It's because they're all out drinking, and I don't want to be like you!" He left shortly after that. I blamed myself. Was it because of what I said?

The memory is bittersweet.

After he was gone, I felt the pressure to be perfect more than ever. I helped my brother keep his room clean. I took out the trash. Hell, as a thirteen-year-old, I did the family's laundry. As long as I made Mom happy ...

Some days, the compulsion was so intense I'd wait until no one was home, and I'd scream.

Now, I get angry because the screams are on the inside of me.

I've got to figure all this out. I have only a few days to tell Mom what's going on, propose to Lacey, and ask Declan if he'll stand for me as best man. Declan having Marisol here is going to bite into the time I want to spend with my brother. Her presence is going to chip away at events I had planned for me and Lacey that would lead up to the grand finale of proposing at sunset on the beach. Jesus. Is it too much to ask that after all these years of trying to be everyone's perfect everything, I just want something to go perfect for me?

I stand on the beach, staring out at the crashing waves as the sun begins to breach the horizon. The weight of responsibility feels heavier than ever. The smooth, cool sand beneath my feet offers me no solace as my thoughts swirl with frustration and regret. As I watch the water crash against the shore, a sense of desperation washes over me. I long for a moment of true peace where I don't overthink every thought. I hoped this week would provide a sliver of happiness that was solely mine and Lacey's. The meticulously planned details, all aiming for perfection, are what I thought would bring true happiness my way. As always seems to happen, the unexpected thwarted my plans. Thank God I have a woman who seems to find joy in the unexpected. Lacey is everything I dreamed of finding in a partner and so much more than I deserve.

"Good morning." A gentle hand touches my shoulder. Turning, I see Lacey, her skin aglow with the warmth of morning light.

"Good morning. How'd you sleep?"

"Not as well as I hoped I would. How about you?"

"Not well at all," I confess.

"Want to talk about it?" Concern shows in her eyes. She sits facing the ocean, and I follow suit. When I'm beside her, she touches my thigh with a comforting hand.

"I think I'm just rehashing everything from yesterday. I'm a little mad at myself. Probably as much as I was at Declan."

"I'm sorry." Her hoarse whisper touches my heart.

"You have nothing to be sorry for. It's me. I mull things over and over until my head hurts and words feel inadequate to mend the rift between us." Her eyes turn soft with understanding.

"Yesterday was yesterday. One thing I know about you is when things haven't gone as planned in your eyes, it messes you up. The thing is, what are you going to do about it?"

"What do you mean?"

"I think the solution is, maybe, instead of trying to make things perfect, you focus on living in the moment.

"I don't know if that's possible."

"I think it is. But I don't think you can do it alone."

I can't decipher if she's offering her own help or proposing someone else's, and if that's the case, I don't want any part of it.

"If you can lower that machismo force field you surround yourself with, you can get someone to help."

That all too familiar guard she's talking about comes around me like a bad habit. "What kind of someone?"

She purses her lips. "You know I'm suggesting counseling—and before you completely rule it out, I'll go with you."

I scoff at the idea. The thought of exposing my frailties to a stranger makes me twitchy. "I'm fine," I state my answer and look away.

"Don't shut me out."

An uneasy silence follows, and my jaw tightens at the idea she's proposing. She inches her foot next to mine until the touch connects us.

"I'm suggesting this because this 'thing' gets you in its grip, and I think it's robbing you of joy." She inhales a deep breath and lets out a sigh, shaking her head in a slight motion as she looks out at the waves. "I don't know, Carter. I know whatever goes on in your head makes you think that life has to be perfect, but it isn't. It's messy and chaotic, and it will never meet your standards because you're always reaching for that next brass ring. Just when you think you've done one thing well, your brain tells you that you could have done better."

I turn away. I've heard enough. I feel exposed.

"Please, stop."

She grabs my arm. Our eyes meet, and the turmoil I feel comes to a halt. Looking into Lacey's eyes is my anchor. The grounding effect of her love is all that I want for the rest of my life. If she were anyone else, I'd feel criticized, but the only thing I feel at the moment is care and concern.

"Life is messy," she says as a tender smile curves her mouth. "It's chaotic but wonderful and so worth all the mishmash. It's in those moments of complete disarray that you muddle through the crap and find something beautiful."

Her words pierce through the turmoil twisting in my mind, and, for a moment, I allow myself to consider what could be instead of what should be. I raise my hand to her cheek, and she smiles.

"Woman, you have no idea what you do to me." Her smile widens, and her emerald eyes shine in the morning light. "Lacey Michelle, you are the only person who can make me see things with more clarity than I believe I have on my own."

She rolls her eyes and shrugs. "It's a gift."

Suddenly, the angst I've been feeling for the better part of the night and morning drifts away with the easy breeze. A chuckle escapes as my hand takes hers. "I don't know if I want it to go away. My brain works

better when I have plans and expectations. It's probably why I did so well when I was in the service."

"Maybe." Her brow hikes. "But for those of us who
love you, it can be a bit suffocating."

"I'll think about it, okay?"

"That's all I'm asking."

Chapter 8

Lacey

My mind is clearer. My heart is lighter. I feel refreshed.

I agonized over having a conversation about the complex topic, and now that it's taken place, I'm relieved.

After we decided to forego our run this morning, I left Carter with Declan on the porch with fresh coffee. Hopefully, they'll enjoy some 'bro time' in the quiet of the morning before joining their mother in the kitchen.

"Good morning, Beautiful. How are you today?"

"It's a little too early to be up and about if you ask me, but here I am," Rose scoffs. "I try to listen to my body when I'm on vacation. You know what I mean, right? I eat when I'm hungry, sleep in a little later ...

vacate my normal, everyday life when I get up at six a.m." She smiles. It's obvious this is a special time for her, despite her lazy morning desire, because the grin crinkles the corners of her eyes. "I see my boys are up. I'm going to make breakfast."

She goes about her business as I sit quietly. I miss my mother, and watching as Rose rummages through the cupboards to get the needed pots and pans reminds me of my and Mom's lazy weekends. Though Rose seems relaxed, the longer I take in her actions, the more I think she looks worn. If I had to take a guess, it would be the aftereffect of yesterday's argument.

"Can I help? You look like you might have had a restless night."

"No, thank you. You're too perceptive, Lacey. The argument left me exhausted. I tossed and turned all night. My boys don't often argue, and I don't like it when they do."

"I spoke with Carter this morning. I think I might have convinced him to speak to someone about his obsessive-compulsive disorder."

She stops what she's doing and gives me a surprised look.

"What? You don't think he has a problem?"

"Oh, I know he has a problem. He's been like this since he was a teenager."

"He told me. He thinks he knows exactly when it started."

"He told you that?" She pauses. "When did he say?"

"Before his dad left. When you two were arguing."

Sorrow flashes in her eyes. "I thought that might have been when. The arguing was gradual, then grew in frequency and intensity. Believe it or not, Carter was a very boisterous and vocal kid. I suppose I was too lost in my own troubles to notice. It wasn't until after my husband left that I did." She grabs a dozen eggs and a loaf of bread. "I'm going to make French toast. Do you like it?"

"I do."

"I don't make it all fancy with Brioche. After their father left, I had to watch my budget. This was a cheap and easy meal, but they thought it was fancy."

"You don't have to tell me. I grew up in a trailer park. My mom did the same."

Rose goes back to her task and places an iron skillet on the stove, concentrating on whipping the eggs with milk and a dash of vanilla. "You know, whenever I mentioned something about him seeing a professional, he pooh-poohed it away. He said he was fine."

"I can only speak from experience, but I wouldn't have wanted my mom to worry about me if I could prevent it. I can't say what will happen, but at least we talked about it."

. . .

"I'D SAY you're a miracle worker, Lacey. Carter' a very determined man."

"You mean hardheaded," I add.

A sputtered laugh escapes Rose. "Yes. Exactly." She pauses. "There's no pulling anything over on you, is there?" She lifts two pieces of egg-soaked bread with a fork and sets them in the frying pan. It sizzles and pops, and Rose turns down the flame and turns her attention to me. "Do you mind me asking if you mind Marisol sharing a few days with us? I'm curious."

"Not at all. I say, the more, the merrier. I think Marisol's gorgeous. I'm hoping she'll pass along a few tips for me. As you know, I'm no fashion plate. Money was always tight when I was a kid. I'd like to look a little prettier."

"I think you're perfect," she immediately blurts out. "And I think you're perfect for Carter."

A sweet, comforting feeling comes over me as my lips erupt into a smile. "You think so?"

"Of course I do." Her expression is tender. "Lacey, the truth is, if I could have picked out a woman who would be perfect for my son, it would be you. You are so swe—"

Rose stops. A bewildered expression shows on

her face as she swoons. I fly to her, terrified she's about to faint, and catch her as she grabs onto the countertop.

"Easy. Easy." I soothe, holding her for a moment. We stay there as a measure of silence falls over us both. I reach over and flip off the knob feeding gas to the burner on the stove. After a few moments, she pushes against it and me, righting her posture.

"I'm okay, Lacey," she says, "I'm good."

Gradually, I loosen my hold on her as she incrementally regains a more solid posture. Embarrassed, she puts distance between us and runs her hand over her hair and down her clothes.

"What just happened? I'm about to go get Carter and Declan."

She pooh-poohs me off with a wave of her hand. "It's nothing. It was a little lightheadedness, is all. It's probably because I didn't sleep well. I'm fine now."

I watch, studying her as she shuffles to the refrigerator and retrieves a container of orange juice. I try to help and grab a glass from the cupboard above me, placing it within her reach on the countertop.

Rose lifts her gaze and presses a quick smile onto her lips. She pours until the glass is half full, then sips it down. I follow her back to the table, where we both take a seat.

"Maybe you shouldn't bother with breakfast today,

Rose. I'll go get Carter. If you're up to it, we can go out for breakfast."

"If you don't mind, I'd like to wait a little while."

"That's fine," I assure her. "We can go whenever and wherever you want. Where is your favorite place to eat around here?"

"There is a little place I love, and they serve a lovely brunch."

"Whatever you want," I assure her.

"I think I'd like to lie down. I have a tendency to overdo it on our first day with grocery shopping and washing dishes. Not to mention my restless night."

"And the boys didn't help with their antics," I add.

"No, they didn't, but I'm used to them." She slowly drains the remaining orange juice, stands, and retrieves a paperback book from a small table over in the corner of the room. She tucks it in the crook of her arm and, as she passes me by, places a hand on my shoulder. I look up, my eyes meeting hers. "Please, don't mention anything to Carter or Declan about this little incident, okay? There's no need to worry them. I'm sure that, after a nap, I'll be good as new."

I eye her warily.

"Lacey, please," she pleads, concern written all over her face.

After a moment of hesitation, I nod, though I'm not happy about agreeing.

"Thank you. When I wake up, I'd love to do brunch if the boys agree. Maybe Declan can get Marisol to join us. It would be nice to get to know her a little better."

"Sounds good," I say softly.

I watch as Rose continues down the hallway to the bedroom door. Once through, the door drifts closed. Somehow, a note, or something like it, cruises on a current of air.

"Rose ..."I call, but she doesn't hear me.

I push out from the table, the chair legs squelching noise against the linoleum floor. As I approach the bedroom, I tiptoe to not bother her and pick up the note from the floor. My eye catches on a bright, bold, red magic marker, and my breath catches in my throat as I make out the words.

Chapter 9

"Mom missed the brunch window. Did you tell her I made reservations for dinner?"

Lacey nods, her mouth full of toothpaste. The soft sound of her toothbrush against her teeth echoes in the small space.

"I could have waited until you were finished." Amused, I watch as she again nods, small fragments of white paste dotting the corners of her mouth. Her eyes meet mine in the mirror, a hint of humor lingering behind their usual sparkle. With a determined rhythm, she completes the task and then turns to me.

"When I went to her room, Rose said she'd be ready soon." She pauses, then her expression grows more serious. "Have you noticed anything different about your mom?"

"Not really. Why?"

She shrugs. "Just asking."

"Have you?" I respond.

"Maybe." She presses a forced smile to her lips, and I feel a check in my gut. "She has seemed a little run down. I thought you might have noticed the same thing."

I stop and search my thoughts but come up with nothing. "I'm usually pretty good at deciphering subtle clues about Mom's moods when I speak with her on the phone, which, as you know, is a couple of times a week. Maybe what you see as fatigue is actually some lingering emotions. Me and Declan ... I think Mom's getting too old for this shit, you know?"

"I guess."

I pull her into my arms. The sunlight that streams through the window dances across the yellow tiles. "I'm sure a nice, relaxed dinner will do everyone good." I give her a quick kiss. "I'm going to go downstairs and see if Mom's ready."

"Okay." She pulls away. "I'm going to change into a sundress. I'll be down in a few minutes."

I grab her wrist and snatch another kiss. "I'll meet you on the porch."

We part in the hallway, and the old wood creaks as I descend the stairs. My mind races with excitement and nerves as I think of what I'm about to reveal. Something I've planned for a while but have shared with no one.

I follow the sound of running water, and the scent of dish soap fills the air. It hits me as I enter the kitchen. Mom smiles at me as she stands near the sink, drying a mug with a towel.

"Mom, can I talk to you out on the porch?" My tone belies my nerves, and concern fills her expression. "It's all good. I promise."

She nods, places the cup down, and follows me outside. The sun still warms the air. I'm hyper-alert and sensitive to sound, so I can detect Lacey's footsteps should she have a chance to discover my secret. I go to the farthest corner, as far away from the door as I can. Birds chirp in the tree behind the house, and summer flowers that enjoy the heat are in full bloom on the trellis beside me. I quickly muster my words and pivot. Mom's eyes go wide as I place my hands on her shoulders.

"I'm going to propose to Lacey," I blurt.

"What? When?" Mom's face lights up with joy and surprise. I peer over her shoulder to ensure that we're safe from Lacey's ears.

"Sometime this week."

"Oh, my gosh. Carter!" Mom's hands come up to her chest and cover the space where her heart resides.

"Shh." I place my finger to my lips. We share a smile, staring at each other as seconds pass, neither of us saying a word as we, instead, let the excitement of this upcoming milestone settle in our hearts. "I had it all planned, but ..."

"Hmm. Now I know why you were so upset with your brother." Understanding dawns in her eyes, and she pulls me into a hug. "Lacey's going to be so happy. I'm excited for you, son."

"I just have to figure out when to do it. I want to do it right, you know?"

"I do, and I'm sorry, honey. I know how important this is to you. Does Declan know?"

"No. I haven't told him yet, but that was also part of my plan; to ask him to be my best man. Now, I don't know when I'll have some time with him." I shrug nonchalantly. "I did have everything laid out, but it's all good, Mom. I'll pull the pieces of this together. I just hope she says yes."

"Of course she will!"

"Mom!" I chuckle. "Shh. She's going to hear you." Concern washes over me as Lacey's observations find the forefront of my thoughts. "And you saying you're sorry is completely unnecessary. It's me who should be sorry. I didn't mean to blow my top. It's just that I had planned to ask him, then Marisol showed up."

"Of course you were upset," she exclaims, then claps her hands together. "You know what? We're not going to let anyone or anything ruin this for you. This is fantastic news!"

I hear movement in the house and put my finger to my lips. "I'll figure it out, but I wanted you to be the first to know."

"I'm so glad you told me." She whispers.

The screen door squeaks. Lacey stands in the doorway as beautiful as ever in a bright yellow sundress. "Is Declan here yet?"

"Not yet, sweetheart," Mom replies as she reenters the house. I follow behind her and take a seat in the rocking chair next to the front door. Mom compliments Lacey's dress, and I watch as the two of them chit-chat. A few minutes later, Declan and Marisol appear.

I watch Marisol as she looks around. She takes in the living room, its well-worn charm seeming to miss her as her posture stiffens.

"Marisol, would you like to join Lacey and me tomorrow? We're going to the outlets."

"What's an outlet?" She asks.

"It's a store that offers discounted prices on designer items," Declan explains.

"I don't need discounts on anything—"

Declan interrupts her, his tone convicting. "Stores like Movado and Michael Kors are there. I'm sure there are other designer shops as well."

"Designers usually come to me," she states with a superior-sounding tone.

"Not everyone has that privilege," he retorts cooly with a hint of impatience.

Marisol says nothing, but her snobbish attitude isn't lost on me.

"I'll treat us all to lunch. It will be fun," Mom adds.

"It will be," Lacey confirms. "And I'd love it if you would help me pick out a few new things. I'm sure you have a perfect eye when it comes to fashion, and I can use a little help. I don't follow the trends, and let's face it; you set them."

Marisol's brows perk as if to confirm Lacey's comment. I dismiss her, mentally brushing her off like she's an annoying bug, then stand, corralling everyone so we aren't late for dinner.

Chapter 10

Lacey

"So, tell us how you came to be a model. We know Declan's story, but I'm interested to hear yours." I open a casual conversation.

Marisol studies me, and then a sly smile hooks the corner of her mouth. "Isn't it obvious?" She frames her face with a wave of her hand.

Rose's smile fades into a tight line, and I feel offended for her. It's apparent Marisol's attitude is off-putting.

"It's obvious you have the look, but don't you have a story? Declan was discovered here, at the beach."

"It was a few years ago. I was on holiday with a few friends. Like Dee-clan, I was on the beach. A man approached me and told me I should model. My father had other plans."

"He was against your modeling? I'm surprised. Surely, he could see the opportunity for his daughter."

"My father is a very powerful man in Columbia. He doesn't like deviation."

The intensity of her comment and her serious expression weigh in the air like a heavyweight. I attempt to lighten the mood.

"I understand that mentality. Carter is a stickler for details, right Rose?" I turn to Carter's mom.

"He is." Her answer is short, and her tone is wary.

"You don't like me very much, do you?" Marisol leans in, folding her arms and placing them on the table.

Rose's eyes narrow in disapproval. "I'm not sure why you would say that. I don't know you well enough to make that determination."

Marisol pushes back. "I can tell."

"Oh, really?" An indignant huff escapes. "How exactly?"

Marisol pushes herself into the corner of the booth and props up her leg, where she places a relaxed arm. "Ladies, honesty is best, no?" She examines us with cat-like eyes. "I'm young and beautiful, and you'll find me in any magazine you choose. This little get-together?"

she emphasizes her point with a circling finger. "It isn't the best use of my time."

Indignation creeps into every ounce of my being, and though I should dismiss her for the bitch she is, I feel compelled to speak.

"You're rude."

"So, I've been told."

I exchange a glance with Rose, who looks equally taken aback by Marisol's brazen attitude. It's clear that Marisol is used to challenging questions, her every movement exuding confidence and entitlement. However, as much as I want to dislike her, there's something magnetic about her that I can't ignore. Maybe it's because she's confident in a way I've never been. I'd be the first to admit that I, like many other women, am insecure about how best to make myself pretty. Hair and makeup aren't skills my mother passed on to me. That slight insecurity makes me wonder how Marisol gained her confidence. The way she carries herself unapologetically, taking up space in a world that would rather confine women, is something I admire.

Before I can stop myself, a query that crosses my mind slips out of my lips. "Why do you do it? It's obvious that you think you're above all this."

Marisol laughs, and the sound is like shards of glass cutting through the air. She leans back against the booth as if she's lounging by a pool rather than sitting in a beachside café.

"Because money is power, and they are paying me an obscene amount of money just to take my picture." With a dismissive smile, she leans back in her seat, seemingly unfazed by the tension she's added to our day.

I look over at Rose, who's struggling to maintain her composure. Although it's clear that Marisol is not used to the company of women, Rose is her opposite, and by the look on her face, takes exception to Marisol's comments.

Before anyone can say anything else, the server arrives with our food. Though the food is tempting, I've lost my appetite. It's faded into the uncomfortable tension that has settled over the table. I try to make the best of it and take a deep breath as I attempt to reconcile the anger that simmers beneath my skin. I pick at my plate, but not her. As we're eating, Marisol looks at Rose and me, her gaze lingering on each of us.

"So, what's next today, ladies?"

Shock ripples through me. I can hardly believe her casual attitude. It's as if her earlier behavior hadn't been a big deal at all.

I turn my head to Rose, whom I have never known as anything other than a kind and considerate woman. Her eyes narrow as a smirk settles on her lips and morphs into an expression I've not witnessed in all the time I've known her. A chill races down my spine.

"Well, dear, I suppose the four of us will continue our shopping excursion. Then we will return to the house, where Declan can see you back to your hotel."

"Four?" A confused look colors Marisol's expression, and she looks around the room. "Is someone else joining us?"

"Oh, no, dear. It's just us." Rose's tone is calm, but her stare holds conviction. "Lacey, me, you, and your insufferable ego."

Marisol's eyes widen, and I see a challenge in her eyes. A flicker of impudence crosses her features before she quickly masks it with a nonchalant smile.

As we finish our lunch, she dramatically inhales a deep breath and lets it out with a sigh. "As you are Declan's mother, I will explain myself; it was not my intention to offend you."

"Well, you see, my dear, you did. I'm not so offended for myself as I am for my friend. You are rude, and I do not care about your lifestyle. What I do care deeply about is the respect and humility that comes with the friendship of women, both of which, it's clear, you do not possess." Rose's expression fills with a determined look. "I'll explain this in as blunt a tone as you used earlier; I don't care for you. Though we may share another meal or two before you slip back into the lifestyle for which you so clearly painted a picture, your presence is not welcome."

Marisol gleefully takes the unspoken challenge. "Aww. I didn't mean to hurt your feelings."

I jolt forward as a sudden urge to slap her rushes through. Rose throws her arm in front of me, seemingly unfazed.

"My feelings are fine. It's good to know where you stand."

My gut twists as Rose calmly pays the bill. As soon as we exit the restaurant, Marisol struts ahead of us with an air of confidence and arrogance. We watch as Marisol makes several purchases, flashing her credit card like a weapon. After suffering her presence as we go in and out of a few stores, I glance at Rose as Marisol puts further distance between us.

"We can go back to the house right now," I say under my breath. Rose's eyes meet mine. "I mean it. We can go right now."

Rose answers with a head shake, so I stuff my anger, the bitter taste of it lingering on my tongue.

Chapter 11

Carter

I wake up to the feeling of Lacey's soft body pressed against mine. The morning light streams through the window. It casts a warm glow over her naked form. She's so perfect. I can't help but reach out and run my fingers through her hair as she stirs.

"Morning," she murmurs, her voice husky with sleep. She stretches, arching her back and pressing her breasts into my chest. I can't help but let out a low growl.

"Morning, baby."

She smiles. "Sometimes, I think that morning is your favorite time of day."

"You have no idea," I respond, my pleasure evident as I press hard against her and capture her lips with mine. Lacey moves closer, her long hair cascading over my chest. I move my hands slowly, inching down her back until they reach her slender waist. She shivers from my touch and presses closer into me, her softness a welcome feeling to start the day.

Heat flares between us as tension builds. She presses her smiling lips against my mouth. "I don't think you need coffee this morning to wake up."

"You should be scared," I counter. I roll over on my back, pulling Lacey with me. Her hips writhe against mine.

She takes my hands and places them on her breasts. I squeeze them gently, and she moans.

Our lips meet, devouring each other as our bodies fuse together. I can feel every inch of her that's pressed against me. My senses rachet into overdrive. Lacey's breath hitches in my ear, and I know that this isn't just about pleasure. We have something much deeper than that. Something we've been building toward for a long time.

A sudden movement catches my eye, and I catch our reflection in the mirror across the room. The same mirror where I fixed my hair on hot summer nights, hoping to catch the eye of a pretty girl to hang out with on the Boardwalk for a summer night. But the girl in my arms is all I've ever dreamed of. All I've ever wanted.

Our bodies twist and turn in a passionate embrace, and I press my throbbing heat into her warm softness. She cradles my aching erection. We grind together, building the anticipation of our release, and I watch with pleasure as Lacey loses herself in the heat of lust. Her eyes drift closed. Her cheeks flush.

With a growl, I push into her. A moan of excitement falls from her lips as my pace increases, my desire for her birthing an animalistic need to claim her. Mark her.

Her sex tightens as an orgasm ripples through her body, accompanied by a cry. It's the catalyst needed for my release to rip free, reminding me that, though she hasn't yet said yes, she's mine.

As I inhale a deep breath, I set my half-empty Corona on the wooden porch railing. The sun is setting, and though I can't see it dipping below the horizon, the sky casts a warm glow over the beach.

"Marisol's been doing this longer than me."

I look over at my brother. "What brought this on?"

"Nothing, but it's obvious you don't like her. There are things about her I don't like but tolerate."

"I don't have to tolerate her. Therein lies the difference. It sounds like she matters to you. She doesn't to me."

"I work hard, Carter. I know you don't think so, but it's work. What I do, how I eat, sleep, and work all mean dollars in my bank account. She took off with little effort."

I shrug. "Maybe she slept her way to where she is now."

"Part of me wonders if that's true, but then, part of me wonders if it was her exotic looks. Whatever it is, I'm nice to her because I have to work with her."

I look over at my brother and see a hint of insecurity. As the baby in the family, he always got a hefty dose of attention. If his confidence takes a hit, it isn't because he lacked security and protection. "One of the things I've always admired about you is your tenacity. You tell yourself you can do something and, damn, if you don't do it and make it easy. You've always done that. Sports. Building stuff. Girls. I've never seen you fail."

His brow quirks. "I have. I guess I just don't focus on the failures. I have this need inside to reach higher and do better."

"Well, she ain't it." The statement falls like a brick.

Mom comes up onto the porch, and Declan jumps up to grab her bags. "Did you have a good time?"

"It was ... interesting."

He follows her into the house just as Lacey returns. I look up at her. "What about you? Did you have a good time?"

"She was the epitome of a diva."

"Can't say I'm surprised." Lacey sits beside me, occupying the seat Declan vacated.

"Not much bothers me, Carter. I tried to give her the benefit of the doubt. Her manicured nails and designer bag didn't bother me, but today ..."

She stops, and I look over at her. Her expression causes me to frown, and I reach inside the little cooler beside me and fish out a beer. I place the wet bottle on the arm of the chair and twist the top off. Lacey takes a sip before continuing.

"She complained about the stores. The staff wasn't helpful enough. At the restaurant, the food wasn't up to her standards. Your mom and I wandered through the rest of the afternoon while Marisol grumbled about having to walk so much in her heels. That woman wore a pinched expression nearly all day."

"I can only guess who we are talking about," Declan interjects and takes a seat beside Lacey. "Give me one of those." He points at Lacey's bottle. I grab another from the cooler and pass it across Lacey, the icy water dripping onto her lap. She brushes it off.

"How you can like that woman is beyond me." She

shifts her gaze forward. "Her ego ... Jesus. I've never met someone so full of herself."

"She's okay with me."

"Well, she wasn't okay today. She was rude to me. She was rude to your mother." She pauses for another sip, collecting her thoughts, and the three of us sit in silence for a moment. "Her clothes might be impeccable and her accessories on point, but that woman has a dark heart. You might want to keep your distance."

"I can't do that."

"Well, you should."

The tension between them is infectious, and a defiant, irritable feeling seeps into my bones.

"Look, I don't know that side of Marisol. She doesn't act like that with me. We work together. Clients love the pair of us, and because of that, I've made more money in the last couple of years than my mom made in practically all her life. I won't jeopardize that, but I also don't want her talking like that to Mom. I'll talk to her."

"She's a nightmare."

"I can see how she could make your day miserable, especially if she behaved the way you say."

I tense up. I don't like the idea of that woman ruining Lacey's—and my mother's—day. My teeth clench, and my jaw tightens. "I don't want her around the rest of the week."

"Neither do I," Lacey agrees. "I don't like the way she acted today and, sorry, Dec, but I just can't see her walking up the Boardwalk with us in those heels—or eating caramel popcorn or getting ice cream—any of the things that Carter tells me are his favorite things about vacation. I mean seriously ..." She turns to Declan. "Can you just imagine her reaction if a seagull shit on her? The woman would have a coronary."

I watch my brother, ready to pounce if he so much as raises his voice. Declan stares at me, then smiles.

"To tell you the truth, the visual of that just popped into my head."

My anger instantly abates as an image of the same scenario enters my thoughts. I savor the moment, and my stiffened spine relaxes into the chair. "I think I'd pay to see that."

Chapter 12

Lacey

Carter's hand is strong and warm, holding mine as we stroll along the shoreline. The sand beneath my feet is like a soft, shifting carpet, each step leaving an imprint that is quickly erased by the incoming tide. The soothing rhythm of the ocean waves accompanies us as we reach a more secluded spot on the beach. As we do, Carter's demeanor shifts.

"Is something bothering you?" I ask.

"No." He quickly responds, but his tone betrays him.

"Why don't I believe that?" I press.

"I don't know. Why wouldn't you?" His words are guarded and tense.

"Because of your temperament. All of a sudden, it's

changed. You clearly were angry with your brother back at the house, and then you seemed calm when you suggested taking a walk. Now, you're tense again." My concern expands as I take in his body language and the tension that's about to crack his jaw.

He looks at me. "My brother was being a brat."

"And now you're acting like one," I blurt. "I'm really trying here. I don't know what's happening in your head, but it's exhausting."

"Oh, nice. Exhausting." He turns away. "That's just great."

"Tell me what's wrong—and don't tell me nothing," I plead.

Carter stops. His piercing eyes bore into my soul, and the intensity of his gaze left me breathless. Our connection reaches every fiber of my being. It's as if he's trying to unravel the secrets in my soul.

Suddenly, the promise I made to Rose weighs on me. Carter's stare makes me feel vulnerable and exposed, yet I find I can't look away. There's this invisible thread that tethers us, pulling us closer together, and I am lost in their depths.

He lets out an exasperated sigh. "I have been keeping something from you. Maybe that's what you detect."

"I knew it. It's bad, isn't it?" I bait him, not willing to spill what I know.

"What? No." He studies me.

"Whatever it is, just tell me," I insist, throwing up my hands.

"Lacey." He stops me. Troubled, he searches my expression and then pulls me close. "Christ ..." His arms tighten around me as his lips brush against my ear. "I'm sorry, baby. This was supposed to be a good week."

"Is it your mom?" I choke on the words, willing him to spill the heartbreak I carry.

He pulls away, putting me at arm's length. A puzzled expression corrupts his handsome face. "She told you, didn't she?"

"Did she tell you?" I repeat.

"Tell me what? That she's happy, I'm proposing?"

My breath rushes out with a whispered word. "What?"

He stops, realizing that he's betrayed himself. Looking away, he rakes a hand through his hair and walks off, frustration pouring from him.

"Carter!" I call after him, suddenly worried I might have given something away while discovering something else. Picking up my pace, I catch up with him. "Stop!"

My hand latches onto his wrist, and he turns. His expression is pained. "I told my mother I was going to propose and, once again ..." Disappointment etches lines in his face. "I guess it's true what they say about the best-laid plans."

Pain fists my heart. I've not exposed Rose's confidence, but I've hurt the man I love.

"Did she tell you?" He sinks my heart with the question, the anguish within them weighing me down.

"No."

With the whispered word, his expression softens. He drops to his knee in front of me. My lungs hold my breath hostage as my heart pounds out a beat so loud I'm sure he can hear. Tears sting the corners of my eyes. As I look at him, the last rays of the sun showcase the love shining within their warm, chocolaty color. I can't let him do this.

Doubts and fears consume me, creeping into my mind and invading my thoughts. The enormity of what lies ahead is daunting. There's something so much bigger than us. I will be there, holding his hand through what he will be facing. Carter's preference for perfection will take over. He'll war with his thoughts. I can't let the months leading up to a wedding conflict with his mother's needs. I'm not sure I could live with the knowledge that his thoughts concerning me and our wedding would occupy any headspace that should be concentrated on Rose.

"This isn't how I wanted to ask you, but it's now or never." He musters a smile. "Will you?"

"I—" My voice cracks in time with my breaking heart and the weight of the obstacles he will face. My heart wants to say yes, but my mind holds me back.

I look away. As I cast my gaze out into the foamy blue expanse and the turbulent waves that mirror the unrest twisting my insides. My emotions tear at me.

Carter rises to his feet, his fingers gently lifting my chin until our eyes meet. "Lacey Michelle, marry me."

In that moment, time seems to stand still. I want this journey with Carter, honestly I do, but I know what obstacles are to come, and my gaze falls away as I shake my head and choke out whispered words.

"I can't."

Chapter 13

Carter

"What? You're turning me down?"

I search Lacey's eyes for an explanation and see a flicker of pain hidden within the blue orbs. An equally distressing look crosses her face before she schools her expression.

Her hand falls out of mine, the warmth of her touch fading like a distant memory. I turn away before she sees the hurt flashing across my face. I force nonchalance in an attempt to mask it. Night is falling, and its impending darkness cloaks me in its inky depths. I struggle for composure, her rejection slicing open my heart as I manage a tight rein on my emotions.

"Carter, please. I don't want to hurt you, but I don't know what to say to make it better."

I shrug off her pity with feigned indifference. "What more is there?"

A crack of thunder steals the sky as I turn away from the woman I thought would be my wife. Her rejection claws into me, finding tender flesh within my psyche to mangle. A storm is brewing, and its impending waves pummel the shore, providing a tumultuous soundtrack for what rages inside me.

"I'm sorry."

"So am I." I walk off toward the house, putting distance between us to cater to my need for silence.

"I didn't mean to hurt you." She calls to me, her voice disappearing in the wind.

"But you did," I mutter. The heady mix of disbelief, anger, and resentment jabs me as I arrive back at the house. I pass by my mother and brother. Their curiosity is evident as Lacey follows silently behind me.

I fling open the screen door with a vengeance that nearly takes it off its hinges and barge through the house to the kitchen, where I help myself to a beer.

"What's wrong?" A look of bewilderment scratches lines across Mom's forehead.

"Does it matter?" I snark before chugging down the cold brew.

"It matters to me."

She watches as I stomp the pedal to the garbage

can and slam the bottle into the bag-lined cavity. Lacey catches my eye as she breaches the doorway, but I quickly catch myself and look away.

"It's my fault," she quietly admits.

"What? How so?" Mom asks in disbelief. Her attention shifts away from me to Lacey.

"I said no."

Silence falls over the room as Declan appears. "What's going on?"

No one speaks as the three of us exchange glances, our gazes ricocheting between us all.

"Well, somebody better spit it out," my brother declares.

I wait, but Lacey says nothing.

"I'll just say my week's getting shittier by the day. The funny thing is, it's not my fault."

"It's my fault." My mother's tone is somber as she pulls out a chair and drifts down into it. Lacey follows behind her, and the two exchange a glance. A sad look slides across Mom's face, and I suddenly feel like something unspoken is weighing down their mood.

Mom looks first at Declan, then me, and at that moment, my heartbeat staggers its beat.

"I have cancer."

The words tumble from my mother's trembling lips, and my world screams from its axis. Cancer. The word echoes through my mind, bouncing around like a cruel joke. I glance over at my brother, his usually carefree expression now corrupted with sadness and worry. There she sat—our rock, our guiding light—looking so small and fragile.

Tears distort my vision as they well up in my eyes, the pelting rain now beating against the cedar shakes. As I wrestle with my thoughts and try to process this news, my thoughts consume me. How can this be happening?

"I would have told you sooner." The sound of Mom's voice wanes, and Lacey squeezes her hand.

"You knew," I convict her with my eyes, and she lifts her gaze.

"I wrote it on a piece of paper with an oncologist's information. The paper fell out of my book, and Lacey found it."

In that moment, I feel a surge of gratitude for her presence as Lacey's eyes fill with compassion and concern.

"I wouldn't have betrayed your confidence, Rose."

"I was going to tell you sooner but didn't want to ruin our time away." Mom's voice holds a tremble.

Tears glisten in her eyes as Lacey comforts her. I'm her son—her blood—and I'm lost for what to say. What's an appropriate response when your world falls to pieces? When six letters form a curse and change your whole life?

"What can I do for you, Mom? What can any of us do?" Declan asks, his palms raised in surrender.

"Make the memory of this week last me for a lifetime." She smiles sweetly, and I swallow a stone of emotion as she sets her sights on me. "Are you okay?"

I nod. It's all I can manage.

The room falls silent for what feels like an eternity, Mom's news shrouding us all with its dark, heavy curtain. I was so self-absorbed I hadn't until this moment noticed the fatigue in her eyes or the way her spirit flickered when it used to shine bright. The unseen, relentless beast attacked when I wasn't looking.

"I'll come down and take you for treatment."

"That won't be necessary," she states with a shake of her head. "It's late stage. I've decided to forego treatment."

"You can't," my brother protests.

"I can, and I am. It's my decision, and I don't want to spend what's left of my time being injected with poison."

"But it'll buy you time."

"I don't need more time to be sick and weak. I'm choosing quality over quantity."

My throat is dry. I struggle to find words. How do you respond when someone you love tells you something like this? My thoughts are all over the place, and so many of them turn to questions. How long does she have? Did I treasure every moment? How will I survive losing the woman who's always been my rock—my guiding light?

I'll respect Mom's decision, but I resent it. I want her here, with us, for as long as possible.

"I will visit the oncologist when we return. Right now, I'm confident I'm making the right decision, but I want to hear all the options before I've totally made my peace with it.

"I'll go with you."

"I'll go with you, too." Declan repeats.

"I'd like to go alone."

"I don't think that's wise," I protest.

"The doctor wants to do a biopsy, but from their test results so far, it appears that it's very invasive."

"I'll come down and go with you."

"Carter, I don't need—"

"I know you don't, but hear me out; a lot is going on in your head. I might catch things that you might miss. I won't interfere with your treatment plan or your decision to forego it. All I'm asking is for the privilege of being there for my mother when she needs me most."

"I'm the same, Mom." Declan's voice drops with a grave tone. "You've always been there for us. Let us be there for you."

"I'll think about it this week. What I would really

like is for the four of us to have fun. To enjoy the remainder of this vacation and make each day the best that we can. There are so many unknowns to face when I get back to Baltimore, but this week is familiar to me. Being at the beach with my boys is the highlight of my year. No matter what I face, I want to savor these memories."

"Rose, I know I'm not family, but whatever you need, whatever I can do ..."

"I know, Lacey, and I appreciate it." Mom pats her hand. "It's nice to have a woman to talk to, and I'm a little too modest to talk to my boys about some things. Some personal things. I know these hulking men aren't boys, but the thought of talking about intimate, feminine things to my sons is unsettling."

Lacey's love for my mother shines through her eyes. Now, I understand better what happened tonight on the beach, and I'm reminded of just how special a woman she is. Still, I am also reminded that I could have been a better man.

Chapter 14

Lacey

I thought I would sleep fitfully after such a stressful evening, but I fell asleep as soon as my head hit the pillow. I don't remember Carter coming in, but the dent in his pillow would indicate otherwise.

Cherishing the solitude, I decide on a plan to make this vacation one all of them will remember. I tiptoe to the door and lock it before grabbing my phone to work out the details.

With my tasks now complete, I throw on my shorts and a T-shirt and go into the kitchen, where there's coffee. No one is inside as I pour a large cup, then I follow the voices outside to the place where my three housemates appear.

I quietly slip into a chair beside Carter and sip the dark brew silently, fighting a smile as they carry on about football. I wait patiently while they each announce their plans for the day.

"I'm going to take Marisol to the airport," Declan says. I'd rather not have to deal with her the rest of the week."

"Thank you, son. I'm not sure she'd have a good time, anyway. I can't picture her playing mini-golf." Rose takes a deep breath and lets it out as she stands. "I'm going to wash this cup, then take a nap. Someone wake me up in an hour or so, okay? I'm tired but don't want to sleep away the days."

"Go rest," Carter says, his tone much softer than it's been in days.

I capture Carter's attention when everyone's done for the evening and have disappeared from the porch.

"Take a walk with me?"

"Sure." He nods.

We walk together hand in hand across the beach until we reach the water, silently enjoying the pleasure of each other's company as we stroll. Then something beautiful catches my eye.

"Look!" I gasp and run ahead of him as a wave throws a piece of sea glass onto the beach. Another wave makes an attempt to reclaim it, but I chase after it and pluck it from the sand. I rinse the beautiful blue piece and run back to Carter to show him my treasure.

Directing his attention to my unfolding fingers, I show him the gem in my hand. "I like it. It's perfect."

"At least something is," Carter mutters, and my suspicions are confirmed that his thoughts are elsewhere.

I purse my lips. "Don't brood."

"Right." He glances at me with sadness in his eyes. "It's not that easy."

As I walk with him, I dig my foot into the wet sand and then fling it back into the water. This puts me a few steps behind him, so I run to catch up and then loop my arm through his. "Are you okay? Last night was heavy."

"No, Lace, I'm not." Emotion cracks his voice as he gives air to my thoughts. "Aside from wanting my mom perfectly well, I also want you to marry me. I get why you turned me down, but I'm not okay with it."

He looks past me, then turns, pointing himself in another direction. I follow.

"I'm going to need you to stop walking."

He ignores me, his stride covering more distance than my short little legs can muster, and I break into a race-walk just to keep up.

He keeps moving ahead as if putting some distance between us will somehow soothe his pain.

"Carter ..." My tone is gentle but persistent.

"What?" He chokes out the word and then stops abruptly, giving me such an intense look that I can almost feel his pain.

"I have a proposal for you."

He rolls his eyes and rears back. "Riiiiiight." His sardonic tone reveals unmistakable thoughts.

"I'm serious," I affirm, my eyes never leaving his.

"And you weren't serious yesterday? That's rich."

I take his arm. I can barely look into his eyes because I know I'm partly to blame for the pain I see there, but I also see a love that won't let me pull away.

"I'm going to make this short and sweet—and it's a true proposal. A bargain. I will marry you."

His brow hikes, and he waits patiently for me to continue.

"I'll do it if you go to counseling."

A smile tugs at the corners of his mouth, and I glimpse the Carter I fell in love with. His smile turns wicked. "Is that a bribe, I hear, Miss? You know you can get into a world of trouble for bribing a cop."

"Maybe I like trouble," I coyly respond.

He steps toward me, closing our distance. "You're a bad girl, Lacey Michelle," his tone is low, like a growl, sending sexy chills down my spine.

"No one but you and my mother have used both my name and tone so effectively," I respond, my voice just a hint above a whisper. "I'll risk a little trouble to make my point."

He hooks his arm around my waist and pulls me tightly against his body, making my breath hitch as desire rushes to my core. "State your case, woman."

I rearrange my thoughts, which tumble like a fast-falling Jenga game the minute his lips come close to mine.

"What's coming up with Rose is going to be hard. I know because of what I went through with my mother."

"And?" his arm tightens.

"You're going to need your head on straight and your thoughts aligned for her. I think I can help."

"How so?" He gives me a wary look.

"Marry me. Marry me now." I take a breath. "My only condition is that you agree to counseling for your OCD."

He gives me a look of disbelief as his warm breath skates across my lips. "You're serious?"

"It's a good proposal," I answer breathlessly. "You won't get a better one."

He studies me, then lets me go, and continues walking along the shore, but this time the water rolls over his feet.

"It's not possible, Lacey. Mom said she is going to see the doctor as soon as we get back."

"Agree, Carter." My tone is firm. "Trust me and agree."

He stops to study me. "You sound like my mother. Hardheaded."

A flicker of happiness rushes through me. "To me, being compared to your mother is high praise that I'll take, and, yes, I am as hardheaded as she is." I'm about to burst from the exciting news, and I hope and pray he'll agree. "We can get married now. Here. I spoke with the pastor at St. Matthew's by the Sea. If we get the marriage license tomorrow, he can perform the ceremony on Friday—if you agree."

His expression is soft and contemplative and in stark contrast with the determined look in his eyes.

An unsure weight lifts from my chest. "What I'm proposing is rushed and chaotic and completely spontaneous, feelings of which you aren't familiar. And I get that you don't like spontaneity, but if you agree, I can offer something to make you happy."

"This Friday? The night before we leave?"

"Why not? We can do it right on the beach with the people who mean the most." I pull my hair over my shoulder and twist it in my hands.

"Who will stand for you?" He asks warily.

"Your mother, of course." The easy confidence rolls off my tongue.

"Woman. You really don't care if things are perfect, do you?"

I give my head a subtle shake. "Nothing's perfect, Carter."

"What about flowers? A cake? Your dress?" A surge of emotion weaves through his tone.

"Since you're Mr. Perfection, I'll leave that to you."

His eyes widen. "You'd let me do that?" he asks hesitantly.

"Why not?" I shrug nonchalantly. Suddenly, the air feels lighter, like it's easier to breathe. "I'll go with your mom and choose a few dresses. I'll let you pick from the selection. You might see the dress but won't see me in it before the ceremony."

"Seriously?"

"Yes. You know my favorite flowers and my favorite flavor cake. What more is there?"

"Rings?"

"There are jewelry stores here."

"Music?"

"We'll use our phone and Bluetooth what we want."

His posture goes slack. "There are other things, like photos and food." He pauses and then looks me dead in the eye. "You're really serious."

"As a heart attack." I smile.

As I lay in Carter's embrace, I can't help but feel contentment. There's a sense of safety in his arms. No one else has ever made me feel so cherished and so loved. His arms are strong and firm around me as if I'm his most precious treasure. Though his controlling tendencies can feel overwhelming at times, when we're like this, they make me feel nothing but protected. I have no reservations about allowing him to arrange our wedding. He always seems to know exactly what I need and, in more ways than one, is more than willing to give it to me.

He pulls me close, and his arm tightens around my waist. I close my eyes, savoring the feel of my body and his spooned together. His lips touch my neck, and my eyes roll back, a wave of desire washing over me.

Warmth radiates from his body as his hard length presses into my backside. I arch back, my head resting against his shoulder as I twist to look at him.

No words are spoken as he captures my chin and crashes his lips to mine. This man loves control, especially in this. I love his dominance. It comforts me.

As he releases my chin, his fingertips roam. He teases my nipple before dipping lower, and I gasp as his hand reaches my core. Plunging deep inside me, a surge of wetness coats his eager fingers, and he plays as my body sings.

"Come for me, Lacey Michelle." His hot breath singes my neck, and I moan into his mouth as my body responds.

"That's my girl. Let it go."

The rumble of his voice trembles my insides, and the room slowly fades away. I'm lost in a sea of pleasure as he takes me wave upon wave.

"You're more than life to me. I'll spend every last day of it devoted to you."

He drags out his movements with measured beats until, ever so slowly, I descend the heights of pleasure. Every muscle relaxes, and every troubled thought rests.

This man is better than anyone I know and so much more than I deserve. With each question and answer, the thought of him creating something beautiful for me brings me joy. After all, I'm surrendering the most important day of my life to someone who thrives on having control. I can see by his expression he's happy. What he thought was unfixable is genuinely within his power to create, and he will.

Chapter 15

Carter

As I stand on the beach shore, sunlight streaming from above, the gentle caress of the ocean breeze ruffles my hair. I can't help but feel a surge of emotions at the site of my one and only, my bride, gliding toward me.

Her feet leave delicate ruts in the sand as she walks toward me draped in white cotton eyelet. Her wedding dress billows as the wind fills its skirt, and she reaches me, surrounded by a marshmallow cloud.

"Hi," I whisper.

"Hi, yourself," she answers, her sapphire eyes glowing. I swallow a ball of emotion that seems to have lodged in my throat. The sun casts her in a golden glow. Tenderly, she holds a bouquet of various flowers in soft, creamy colors. Their sweet fragrance mixes with the salt air, creating a memorable, intoxicating scent.

Her eyes meet mine and are filled with so much love and happiness that it takes my breath away. She responds when I reach for her hand, the warmth of her touch grounding me in this present moment. The sound of the waves is pure bliss as they toss and tumble before their final crash. What I need to make me happy stands beside me; my Lacey, whose eyes sparkle with joy.

"I would normally start this service with a 'dearly beloved, we are gathered here today, but I can see that this couple has their dearly beloved around them. When Lacey approached me the other day, I wasn't sure about performing a ceremony without premarital counseling and all the other things the church recommends. I feel no check in my spirit as I look upon these two. On my reputation as a man of God, I can confidently say there's love here. We are standing in the presence of two people and, joined as one, they'll be an indomitable force." He pauses.

"Carter, do you take this woman, Lacey, to be your wedded wife?"

"I do."

"And do you, Lacey, take Carter to be your wedded husband?"

"I do."

The pastor pronounces us man and wife, and a profound sense of peace instantly settles within me.

"You may kiss your bride."

I turn to my new wife, her eyes shining with love and anticipation, and claim her mouth with a possessive yet gentle kiss.

It's a merging of souls and kindred spirits, and, in that moment, the world falls away. Mom and Declan applaud, and we break apart, our eyes locked in a promise of forever.

We go back to the house to celebrate our union, and I feel content for the first time in my life. This is where I was always meant to be, with Lacey by my side, celebrating our new life together with champagne and her cake combination.

"I see chocolate," she says lyrically.

"Your favorite. Yellow cake with milk chocolate icing."

"It's perfect." Her wide smile nearly reaches her eyes, and her joy makes her shine like the sun. Seeing her so happy and obviously in love fills me with a sense of contentment unlike anything I've known. I look down at the band on my finger, its presence confirming our tethered connection.

Then, there's Mom.

I glance over at my mother, who's beaming as she

stands between her new daughter and the minister. She's so brave, laughing in the face of the beast that lives inside her. I don't know what the future holds, but I'll encourage her to eat the cake and drink the champagne for now. If I've learned anything this week, it's that tomorrow isn't promised.

I catch Lacey's gaze. "I'd like to propose a toast to my new husband," she lifts her glass high in the air. "When they say someone broke the mold, it means no one like them. My husband is that person. He's steadfast, loyal, and protective of those he loves. To you, Carter, and to a long life together."

I take a sip, then mimic her actions. "She's a hard act to follow, but I'll try." I raise my glass. "To you, Lacey Sinclair. You own my every thought and every heartbeat. This is our perfect beginning."

no perfect man

IMPERFECTION SERIES BOOK 1

PREVIEW

Award-winning Author
DD LORENZO

Preview Chapter 1

Declan

Gotta love the view.

    I had watched her for days. She was a natural beauty and seemed completely unaware of me. Almost ethereal, she was effervescent, sparkling, and floating in the sunrise scene before me. A woman who was the epitome of my personal definition of beauty. She certainly didn't look like the manufactured images I was used to from Madison Avenue. Walking with an air of innocence, she had me hooked from the first moment I saw her.

    As she walked along the shoreline, I simply sat back and enjoyed the show. Nothing more beautiful competed for my attention and nothing rivaled my view of her.

The summer season had come to a close, taking with it the manic pace that accompanied thousands of vacationers. Fall at the beach was such a quiet time of year. I was the beautiful girl's one-man audience. Watching her had quickly become my favorite way to spend the morning.

She always walked at sunrise and I was an early riser. Always had been. It fit well with my lifestyle and maintaining my body as a marketable product. It also meant ungodly hours of working out. I'd been slacking since I was on vacation, but still I woke up before the crack of dawn.

I came here to get away from the city. The New York fashion industry was a demanding mistress and early morning gym time was a necessity for guys like me. We all struggled to fight the effects of time. There wasn't a person I knew in the industry who didn't know the rules of strict diet and exercise. It was a crucial fact of life if we wanted to ensure a steady stream of income. Being a model in a fiercely competitive field, I'd stayed at the top longer than most, maintaining the status of male supermodel. I was lucky enough to be represented through New York's prestigious Bella Matrix agency. Though I was nothing more than a handsome face and tight body to the world, in my eyes I was a bona fide CEO, President, and Chairman of the Board. My company was me: Declan

Sinclair. The bricks were stacked with my blood, sweat, and tears, while my spirit was the number one employee. I'd worked damn hard to build it from the ground up and probably sold some of my soul along the way. I'd come to New York with a dream and, in my field, had become the *cream of the crop, top of the heap,* just like the song said—at least for the time being. With washboard abs and a killer smile, I'd been featured in hundreds of magazines and had even seen my face on fifty-foot billboards in the middle of Times Square. I hawked everything and anything that would make a buck. Fragrance, underwear, and fine men's suits had proven to be the most lucrative; I'd made more money in six years than most people see in a lifetime. I was living life on my terms, and now that I could go anywhere, do anything, and buy what I wanted, my choice was to have a place of my own where I could escape. I went where I had my best memories—Ocean City, Maryland. *Home* was a good place. The house had been renovated and decorated in my taste and it was right on the beach. It had been one helluva challenge. The entire structure was saltwater seasoned, frayed, and busted when I found it, but I knew from seeing it over the years that it had two important things going for it: it had endured the test of time and it still had good bones. The realtor told me I was out of my mind for wanting it, but I didn't agree. She didn't think the house was worth the time or effort, not to mention the money it would take to restore it. Secretly, I wondered if some hotel was waiting in the wings to make a nice offer for the property and knock it down. But I persisted because I saw past the old girl's wrinkles and into her soul. She was a true beach beauty. All she needed was someone to take away the dilapidation and give her a facelift. Now, after months of painstaking work and a talented construction crew, she was more than stunning. All she needed was a little love.

The beach was my escape when I needed to get away from the craziness of New York. When I needed some space to think. The atmosphere was conducive for the peace I craved and was the perfect place to hear my own thoughts. The white sandy beach of Maryland's Eastern Shore was the perfect place for me to put down roots; and I was content here. There was absolutely nothing that could compare to an ocean view. Instead of traffic, I heard the peaceful song of seagulls in the morning. The majesty of a coming storm quieted the static in my mind. The massive front porch was my favorite part of the house. Though it had rickety railings and was missing a few boards when I looked at the place, it was what sold me. From the moment I placed my foot on the timber, I got a reaction. The wood moaned beneath my feet and, when I put my hand on the thick post and looked out, I was hypnotized by the panoramic view of water, sky, and sand. Tranquil washes of color assaulted my desensitized perception of beauty and sedated me better than any drug high. I was inspired by those hues and asked that the colors dictate the interior. The relaxed furnishings reflected the real me and the relaxed vibe that I wanted to create. I gave her a name, since most of the buildings in the area had been christened with one. *The Seaductress.* She was all mine. The first place I truly felt at home. On the morning after I finally moved in, I was enjoying the morning breeze and a cup of coffee. No rushing around, no agenda. After living in such a pretentious and fast environment, it was the best feeling I'd ever known.

Until her.

Adjusting for a better view, I switched my cup to the other hand and brushed the sand from my feet as I crossed my legs and rested my ankle on my knee. The stunning dark-haired beauty took delicate steps, leaving indentations behind her in the wet sand. Her gentle strut was prettier than any I'd seen by a runway model during Fashion Week. She was my new addiction.

I sank into one of the house's original oversized

Adirondacks. Enjoying the scrape of the rough wood as it scratched my back, I savored my little slice of heaven and stretched out my legs. I didn't know how I would do it, but I wanted to know everything about her. She appeared each morning around the same time, seemingly lost in her own world. She didn't notice me, which was a good thing. I knew what it was like to be stalked. But from the carefree way she walked, I was certain she'd never known the stress of living life under the public's microscope or the prying eyes of the blood-thirsty press. Sometimes I wished that I could go back to that anonymity. Although having the attention of the world was exciting when I was eighteen, it had lost its flavor over the years. Everything I did, no matter how large or small, was subject to public scrutiny. Every day spent in a major city, from the moment I stepped outside or stood in front of a hotel, people who wanted to know me just a little bit more watched me. *The same way I feel about her.*

Ocean City was the perfect place to escape their prying eyes and was the last place the paparazzi would think to look for me. I had left no contact information at the agency when I told them I was going on vacation. *My secret.* There was only one person who knew how or where to reach me, and that was my brother, Carter. He'd found his own piece of heaven in the mountains of Deep Creek Lake. Although our careers took us on different paths, this house meant as much to him as it did to me. It held memories for both of us and that was just one more reason why I had wanted to buy it. When Mom brought us to the beach for vacation after Dad left, things were hard. Mom used up what was left of her savings to bring us on vacation, so there wasn't any money for carnival rides. Carter and I made our own fun. While Mom sat under an umbrella reading her book, we alternated jumping waves and playing Nerf football. Mom always brought us to the same spot on the beach, right in front of this house. At the time, there was an old lady who sat on the porch in a rocking chair. She always smiled and waved. One time we overshot the ball and it landed on her property. We thought for sure we were in trouble because she got up from her chair and went in the house. Neither one of us wanted to tell Mom, but we walked up the beach until we were right at the house. We thought we could sneak up and grab our ball before the old lady came out. Just when Carter stepped onto the porch, the old lady came out the door. We expected to get yelled at, but instead she asked us if we wanted some cookies and held out a plate of chocolate chips. Mom had turned around to see where we were and the lady waved at her. "I want to give the boys cookies. Is that alright?" Mom nodded and watched. We took one in each hand and Carter stuck the football under his arm. Once we thanked her, we went back to the blanket next to Mom. I never forgot her or the house. Back then I had told Carter that when I grew up, I wanted to buy the house from that old lady. Usually, he would punch me in the arm, like older brothers do when their younger brothers say something stupid, or at least mock me and tell me to, "Dream on." That day he didn't. *Little did we know.*

The warm feeling instigated by my memory continued as I observed her steps. She was getting closer and I grew impatient to see her better. As she drew nearer, I saw her in more detail. Long hair, as dark as midnight, nearly kissed her waist. The sun had been playing hide and seek all morning with gray clouds that grew darker by the minute, but it still caressed her shoulders with golden rays. I found myself smiling at the simplicity of her dipping her feet in the frothy edges of the waves as they pulled back from the sand to the sea. The escalating wind whipped the edges of her gauzy shirt. It covered a white camisole, and as it fell from her shoulder, my fingers twitched to return the strap to its rightful place. She was sexier in her innocence than any woman who purposely put on a show.

As she drifted closer, I brought my feet up to rest on the railing and sunk down so she wouldn't notice me for the voyeur I'd become. She was closer than she'd been on any other morning and I was thrilled to finally see her more clearly. Cheeks that were fuller than was acceptable by model standards only made her more beautiful to me. She was stunning in her simplicity and captivating in her oblivion. It was like watching a dream in my head come to life. *Beautiful girl.* The brainwashing of America obviously hadn't tainted her. The photoshopped images in television commercials and magazines had set an unattainable standard for most women. She sat down and wiggled her butt back and forth, getting comfortable in the sand. I leaned forward and traced her curves with my eyes. I craved to touch a woman who was real. I was sick of scrawny women; looking at her made my fingers throb with a desire to feel more flesh than bone. The wind picked up strength and her curls caught against her throat, making my mouth water. She leaned her head back and wiped under her eyes with the back of her hand. *Was she crying?* I didn't have time to expand on the thought, as she stood nearly as fast as she sat down. A rumble of thunder broke through the silence. She grabbed her shoes and a Dunkin' Donuts cup with one hand and wiped her face again with the other. I didn't have time to make myself inconspicuous when she looked right at me. Her eyes locked with mine. *Shit!*

She smiled. My chest squeezed. It happened so fast that I couldn't think. I felt like a googly-eyed high school kid as I returned her sweet expression with a wide grin. As the storm closed in, she ran. My brain registered everything in slow motion like the beginning of the show *Baywatch*, except better. I took in everything about her, including the tiny grains of sand that launched into the atmosphere as she ran toward me.

Preview Chapter 2

Aria

I'd have been blind not to see him. Truth be told, I'd noticed him out of the corner of my eye. One morning while I was walking on the beach, I took a sip of coffee and there he was. It was hard to look away. I kept the cup pressed to my lips so I could continue staring without drawing too much attention to myself. I was stunned. He was so damn gorgeous. I think I scalded my tongue. Thinking back, it's a wonder I was able to swallow. He was better looking than a Greek god. His arms were raised above his head and his jeans hung low on his hips. He was completely stretched out holding onto a beam overhead and my stomach flipped. My reaction to him instantly replaced the numbness that had been suffocating me. I tried to run away from it after the death of my dad and I'd been lost in my grief, oblivious to so much for so long. The sight of this guy jumpstarted my body, reminding me what it was like to feel. Tingles of excitement bounced around my insides like a silver ball in an arcade machine. I missed my dad so much that grieving had become a habit. *But wow! This man!* Just the sight of his slick perspiration-kissed muscles made my pulse race. Whatever he was doing—chin-ups, pull-ups—*whatever*, it drenched my dormant libido with hormonal activity.

I thought he might have noticed me staring, but I wouldn't have been disappointed if he hadn't. That particular day wasn't one of my best. I looked like hell. After tossing and turning all night, I'd debated whether or not to go out that day; but knowing that the fresh air always helped to lift my mood, I went to the ocean's edge. My aunt and uncle had graciously extended an invitation for me to spend some time at their beach house. They sensed that I needed to get away after my father's passing and I happily accepted. I thought that being in a place I loved and experiencing the quiet of the off season would help me to process his death and get back to the business of living. But being alone at *The Skipjack* proved to be both a blessing and a curse. Bittersweet memories followed me through every room. One night I had gotten a drink from the refriger-ator. As I leaned against the sink twisting the cap off of the water bottle, an image of my father materialized. He was standing at the stove making spaghetti. He never cooked at home, but vacation brought out his inner Julia Child. He even tried to sound like her, his voice high, shrill, and amusing. He imitated her, relating each step aloud in a singsong manner as he seasoned the ground beef. Everyone laughed at his uncharacteristic display. The memory warmed me as I showered, changed, and snuggled into bed, the recollection fresh in my mind. Thoughts of Daddy engulfed me like a fluffy down comforter. The pleasant feeling was short lived unfortunately, because being near the ocean during a change of seasons meant unstable atmospheric conditions. The sounds could instantly morph dreams into nightmares and just as I slipped into unconsciousness, a squall blew in. It had never bothered me before, probably because I was usually there with so many people. The unfamiliar house noises scared me, keeping me awake until the storm passed and the sounds mellowed. My frayed nerves were nothing more than splinters by then and as soon as the dark night traded its colors toward morning, I threw on some clothes and headed for the ocean. I knew that a nice long walk could shake the apprehension that clung to me like a humid summer afternoon. I craved the restoration I found only when lingering by the sea. The salt air penetrated my uncomfortably tight chest, soothed my tortured soul, and layer by layer, peeled away my grief and pain. The ungodly numbness fell away in the sea breeze and the heaviness that constantly crushed my spirit dissipated under radiant skies.

Although I wanted to remember Daddy and all the good times, when I was at the house, ghosts and loneliness pierced my memories with sorrow. But the ocean air had a way of cleansing me and morning walks became part of my routine.

Today I stopped on the boardwalk to get my usual coffee before making my way down the beach. I was pleasantly surprised to see that the man I'd noticed previously was once again sitting on the porch. After weeks of self-imposed isolation, I was suddenly thirsty for conversation. I had no idea how to approach him though. I wasn't one of those girls who was bold enough to just walk up and say *Hi. I'm Aria.*

Then fate handed me an opportunity by cracking open the sky.

Huge drops littered the beach as I half walked, half ran, toward him. I needed shelter and he was right in front of me. The sky thickened in woolen shades of gray and a chill whipped through the air, turning the sand from friend to foe. A loud rumble of thunder at my back propelled me and I broke into a jog. I was almost there when the clouds split apart and poured sheets of rain. I was the tallest thing on the beach, so when a bolt of lightning threaded in a jagged line through the air, I felt the electricity and nearly jumped into his arms. His muscles flexed under his shirt as I grabbed his arms to keep from slipping. The material stretched tightly across his firm chest. His gaze met mine as he held onto my waist. *Sweet Lord!*

The feel of him rendered me speechless. I could barely put together a coherent string of words. Operating on autopilot, I extended my hand. I didn't even recognize my voice because it had gotten lost in whispered shallow breaths. Looking into his handsome face, the words tumbled naturally from my lips.

"Hi. I'm Aria."

Get No Perfect Man on your favorite book site.

DD Lorenzo is an award-winning author of Women's Fiction and Romantic Suspense novels. She loves coffee, long lunches with good friends, and fresh flowers to balance her obsession with anti-heroes. You can find her most days plotting and planning her character's lives from her beach house on the Delaware shore.

To stay updated with DD's books, please visit her website at www.ddlorenzo.com and sign up for her newsletter. Want the inside scoop? Join DD's reader group, DDs Diamonds, at www.facebook.com/groups/ddsdiamonds

Stay connected with DD

Website:

www.ddlorenzo.net

facebook.com/ddlorenzo.author

instagram.com/ddlorenzobooks

pinterest.com/ddlorenzo

bookbub.com/authors/d-d-lorenzo

amazon.com/DD-Lorenzo/e/B00GA5ARJ8

goodreads.com/D_D_Lorenzo

Other Titles by DD Lorenzo

The IMPERFECTION Series

No Perfect Man

No Perfect Time

No Perfect Couple

No Perfect Secret

No Perfect Woman

No Perfect Beginning: An IMPERFECTION Series Prequel

The ROCK HILLS Series

Boundless Hearts: A ROCK HILLS Origin Story

Bone Dust: Rock Hills Book 1

Standalones

Indiscretion

(An Aleatha Romig's Infidelity World Novella)

Heels, Rhymes, & Nursery Crimes

(A multi-author series)

Twinkle, Twinkle Little Star: Fragile Flower to Femme Fatale